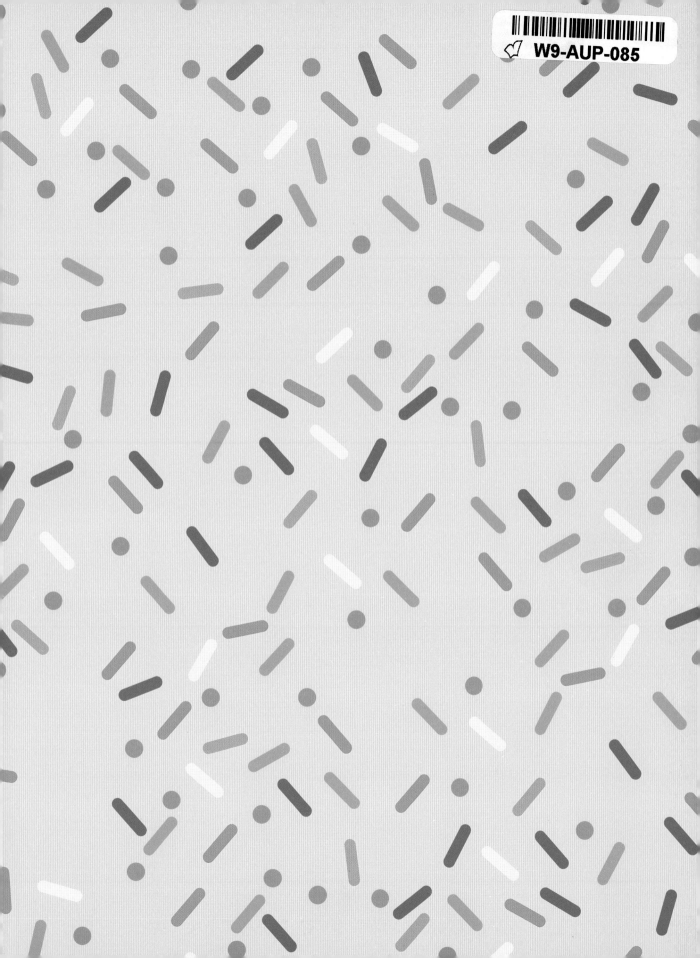

www.mascotbooks.com

Alycat and the Thursday Dessert Day

For more information, please contact:
Mascot Books
620 Herndon Parkway #320
Herndon, VA 20170
info@mascotbooks.com

Third Printing. This Mascot Books Edition printed in 2020.

Library of Congress Control Number: 2016910280

CPSIA Code: PRT0320C
ISBN-13: 978-1-63177-744-8

Printed in the United States

Alycat
and the
Thursday Dessert Day!

By Alysson Foti Bourque

Illustrations by Chiara Civati

For Izzy and Carter, who inspire me.

For my parents, who believe in me.

For Doug, who encourages me.

- AFB

Alycat pounced down the stairs and onto the kitchen chair with a pep in her step and a spring from her tail.

"It's dessert day at school today!"

It was Thursday, the second-to-last day of the school week. Alycat had been looking forward to this day her whole life—well, her whole week.

"Make sure you eat all of your breakfast," Mom said. "You wouldn't want dessert to be your only meal today."

"Well, that wouldn't be so bad," Alycat snickered as she scraped the last scoop of oatmeal out of her bowl.

"I wonder if the dessert will be ice cream, **fudge Popsicles,** or those Popsicles with ice cream in the middle," said Alycat.

"I **LOVE** those!" Bugsy announced.

"Well, it's too bad that your class only gets plain Popsicles until you get to be as old as me."

"They're still yummy, sis," Bugsy said proudly. "Don't you think, Mom?"

"Plain Popsicles, ice cream Popsicles, and fudge Popsicles are all great desserts," Mom said as she picked up the empty breakfast bowls from the table.

"What about pOpcorN Popsicles?" Bugsy joked.

"Yuck! Not unless they're covered with extra butter, sprinkles, or chocolate!" Alycat said as she licked her lips.

"That would be mighty tasty," said Dad.

"The bus is here!" Mom called. "Get your backpacks on! Love you to the moon and back! And have a great dessert day!"

Alycat and Bugsy scrambled out of their chairs and yelled, "Love you to the moon and back, Mom and Dad!"

With their backpacks on and shoes tied, Alycat and Bugsy ran out the front door with a hop, skip, and leap all the way up the bus steps.

SCHOOL BUS

"**Welcome, kittens!**" the bus driver announced. "All aboard and take your seats!"

The kittens were off to school, and Alycat stared dreamily out of the window, watching the trees and mailboxes flash by as they passed. The faster the bus went, the blurrier the trees became. Alycat imagined the trees becoming Popsicles as the orange fall leaves dropped to the ground.

When it was finally lunchtime, Alycat was last to the lunchroom. She had been daydreaming about an orange Popsicle with a sweet ice cream center and missed the bell ringing.

Even while she waited in the lunch line, she thought about how cold the Popsicle would taste on this hot day and how chewing on the end of the stick would help her **wiggly** tooth fall out.

"Next!" shrieked the lunch lady. Alycat slid her tray down the line, watching as each of her friends grabbed a dessert at the end. *There they are!* Alycat thought excitedly. The Popsicles were so cold, ice was falling off their wrappers.

"I can taste it now!" Alycat exclaimed. But
when she opened the icebox, there were
NO POPSICLES LEFT!

"They're all gone!" cried Alycat.
"How can that be?"

Alycat's teacher suggested she could get a Popsicle from the younger kittens' icebox.

"I can't," whined Alycat. "They're plain. If my Popsicle doesn't have ice cream in the middle, I will not eat it!"

Tears filled Alycat's eyes, and she hissed with disappointment.

"I've dreamed of this day my whole life—well, my whole week!" Alycat said sadly.

"I'm sorry, Alycat. If you want a Popsicle, you must get what's left from the other kittens' side," her teacher explained.

"Remember—you get what you get and you don't throw a fit."

"I don't want any dessert at all," declared Alycat, quickly taking her plate. Tears rolled down her furry cheeks as she watched the other kittens finish their lunch and start on dessert.

Spotty saw Alycat in tears and quickly finished his dessert.

"Do you want to come play outside on the jungle gym, Alycat?" Spotty asked.

Alycat wiped her tears and shouted, **"I'll race you!"**

Spotty and Alycat ran as fast as they could to the playground.

"You shouldn't be so sad about the dessert," Spotty said. "It was the same old dessert we have every Thursday. Nothing exciting."

"Thanks for trying to make me feel better, Spotty, but those Popsicles are really good!"

"Yes, but it wouldn't hurt to have something different every once in a while."

The bell rang, and the kittens ran inside to start their math class. But Alycat was still sad about how she missed dessert day.

The day went by and school came to a close. Alycat and Bugsy got off the bus and headed inside to greet their mom.

"How was dessert day?" Mom asked excitedly.

"Great," said Bugsy. "I had a blue Popsicle, and it was so cold!"

"I didn't have any dessert," Alycat protested. "The lunchroom ran out of ice cream Popsicles, and I didn't want anything else!"

"You shouldn't let that stop you from getting another kind of dessert," said Mom. "Sometimes change is good."

"I know, Mom, but it just wasn't fair!"
Alycat moaned as she ran up to her room.

All evening she wished for a dessert as delicious as the ice cream Popsicles but knew she didn't have anything at home that came close.

"I know!" Alycat shrieked. "I can make my own Popsicles!"

Alycat ran to her craft set and pulled out ten Popsicle sticks and pounced into the kitchen.

She popped a bag of pOpcOrN in the microwave and poured it into a large bowl. Next, she took a large plate and filled it with chocolate syrup. Alycat dipped the Popsicle sticks in the chocolate syrup and then rolled the sticks in the popcorn bowl until she had enough popcorn stuck. Lastly, Alycat sprinkled RAINBOW sprinkles onto the popcorn and voilà!

"POPCORN Popsicles!" she squealed.

Bugsy heard the commotion and ran into the kitchen.

"Where did you get those popcorn Popsicles?" he asked. "I want one!"

"I made them! I'll make you one too!" Alycat said excitedly.

"These are great, sis!" Bugsy said as he gobbled up the last bite. "You should make a bunch for your class for Show and Tell tomorrow!"

"That's a great idea!" agreed Alycat. "Everyone will love them!"

The next day Alycat brought the popcorn Popsicles for everyone in her class. They were a big hit!

"I'm glad you were willing to try something new," said Alycat's teacher.

"These are the best Popsicles I've ever tasted!" said Spotty. "I'm so glad we get to have dessert day again today."

"Me too," said Alycat as she ate the last piece of popcorn from her stick.

Just then, Alycat felt a tiny pinch in her mouth.

"My tooth!" Alycat screamed. "It fell out!"
The other class kittens gathered around to see the excitement.

"I will use my tooth fairy money to buy more Popsicle sticks
and make more desserts!" Alycat announced.

"Great idea!" said Spotty. "Thanks for bringing a new dessert today!"

"Anytime!" said Alycat. "I love dessert day! Trying new things is exciting!"

Alycat's Popcorn Popsicles

Ingredients

1 bag plain popped popcorn
1 cup brown sugar
1/4 cup honey
1/2 cup light corn syrup
1 stick salted butter
1/2 tsp baking soda

Decorations

Melted chocolate chips
Rainbow sprinkles
Popsicle sticks or skewers

Directions

Grease a large mixing bowl and baking sheet with non-stick cooking spray.

Cook the popcorn according to the packaging directions and pour into mixing bowl.

Combine the brown sugar, honey, corn syrup, and butter in a saucepan over medium heat. Heat and stir until the butter is melted. About 5 minutes.

Once melted, turn heat to medium high and bring to **boil**, stirring constantly for 10 minutes. Turn the heat off and immediately stir in baking soda. Carefully pour over popcorn and stir until popcorn is coated.

Cool until mixture can be handled. Grease hands with butter and shape popcorn into balls about 3 1/2 inches in diameter. Place the popcorn balls onto the baking sheet and pierce with the craft stick or skewer.

Drizzle with melted chocolate and cover with rainbow sprinkles. **ENJOY!**

About the Author

Alysson Foti Bourque is the author of the *Rhyme or Reason Travel* series and the *Alycat* series. She received a Bachelor of Arts degree in elementary education from the University of Louisiana at Lafayette, and a law degree from Southern University Law Center in Baton Rouge. After practicing law for six years, Alysson traded in writing trial briefs for writing children's books.

When Alysson is not writing stories for her children, she takes pride in working in her garden, caring for her pets, serving her community, and volunteering at her children's school. She believes there is an Alycat in all of us, encouraging our imaginations to guide us to new opportunities and adventures.

Love Alycat?

Check out the plush doll available for purchase on
alycatseries.com and mascotbooks.com!

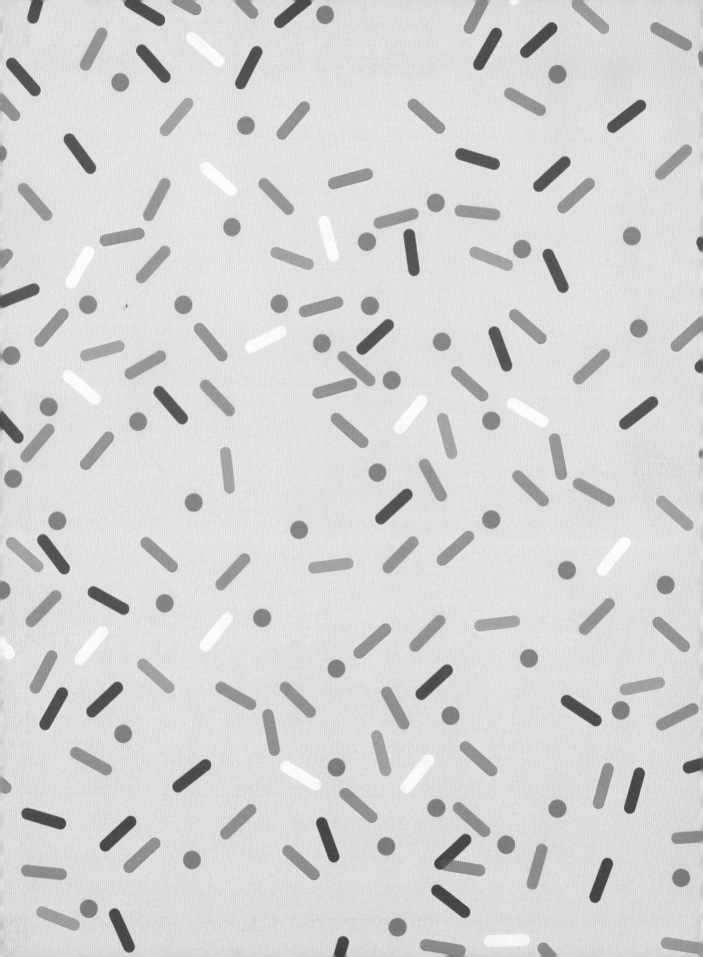